THE POSSIBILITIES

By the same author

Stage Plays
Cheek
No One Was Saved
Alpha Alpha
Edward, The Final Days
Stripwell
Claw
The Love of a Good Man
Fair Slaughter
That Good Between Us
The Hang of the Gaol
The Loud Boy's Life
Birth on a Hard Shoulder
Crimes in Hot Countries
No End of Blame
Victory
The Power of the Dog
A Passion in Six Days
Downchild
The Castle
Women Beware Women (with Thomas Middleton)
The Possibilities

TV Plays
Cows
Mutinies
Prowling Offensive
Conrod
Heroes of Labour
Russia
Credentials of a Sympathizer
All Bleeding
Heaven
Pity in History

Radio Plays
One Afternoon on the 63rd Level of the North Face of the Pyramid of Cheops the Great
Henry V in Two Parts
Herman with Millie and Mick
Scenes from an Execution

Poetry
Don't Exaggerate; Desire and Abuse
The Breath of the Crowd
Gary the Thief/Gary Upright

Film
The Blow

PLAYSCRIPT 113

THE POSSIBILITIES

Howard Barker

JOHN CALDER · LONDON
RIVERRUN PRESS · NEW YORK

First published in Great Britain, 1987, by
John Calder (Publishers) Limited
18 Brewer Street, London W1R 4AS

and in the United States of America, 1988, by
Riverrun Press Inc.,
1170 Broadway, New York, NY 10001

Copyright © Howard Barker 1987

All performing rights in these plays are strictly reserved and application for performance should be made to:

Judy Daish Associates Limited
83 Eastbourne Mews, London W6 6LQ

No performance of these plays may be given unless a licence has been obtained prior to rehearsal.

ALL RIGHTS RESERVED

British Library Cataloguing in Publication Data

Barker, Howard
 The possibilities — (Playscript; 113).
 I. Title
 822'.914   PR6052.A6485
 ISBN 0-7145-4135-4

No part of this publication may be reproduced, stored in a retrieval system, or transmitted in any form or by any means electronic, mechanical, photocopying, recording or otherwise, without the prior permission of the copyright owner and publisher.

Any paperback edition of this book is sold subject to the condition that it shall not, by way of trade, be lent, resold, hired out, or otherwise disposed of, without the publisher's consent, in any form of binding or cover other than that in which it is published.

Typeset 9/10pt Times by Artset (London) Limited
Printed in Great Britain by Hillman Printers (Frome) Ltd, Somerset

CONTENTS

1. The Weaver's Ecstasy at the Discovery of New Colour — 7
2. Kiss My Hands — 13
3. The Necessity for Prostitution in Advanced Societies — 17
4. Reasons for the Fall of Emperors — 23
5. Only Some Can Take the Strain — 31
6. The Dumb Woman's Ecstasy — 39
7. She Sees the Argument But — 47
8. The Unforeseen Consequences of a Patriotic Act — 53
9. The Philosophical Lieutenant and the Three Village Women — 59
10. Not Him — 65

*THE WEAVER'S ECSTASY AT
THE DISCOVERY OF NEW COLOUR*

CHARACTERS

THE WOMAN
THE MAN
THE GIRL
THE BOY
FIRST SOLDIER
SECOND SOLDIER

A FAMILY OF TURKS are weaving a rug. The noise of a bombardment. They concentrate.

THE WOMAN. My nerves ...! I try, but my nerves ...!
THE MAN. I am ahead of you now ... Now, because of your nerves, I must wait.
THE WOMAN. The needle goes all —
THE MAN. The needle goes where you command it. *(A shell lands).*
THE WOMAN *(throwing down the needle).* **You see, my nerves!**
THE GIRL. It's God's will, where the shell falls, and our nerves can neither encourage nor deflect it.
THE WOMAN. I know ... I know ...
THE MAN. Pick up the needle.
THE GIRL. If we stop for the shells, when the siege is over and trade picks up, we shall be short of stock.
THE WOMAN. These are all things I know.
THE GIRL. I know you do. I am not lecturing you.
THE MAN. There are many terrible things, but the worst thing of all is to be short of stock.
THE WOMAN. I know. Even my death would not be worse.
THE BOY. Nor mine.
THE WOMAN. Nor yours, either. But I cannot hold the needle when these —
THE BOY *(looking).* Our army is retreating!
THE MAN. God has his reasons.
THE BOY. But the Christians will enter the city!
THE MAN. Then it was obviously God's intention. *(A shell falls. There is a cry near. Pause).* You have stopped. Why have you stopped?
THE BOY. I should take a rifle from a dead man and I should —
THE MAN. **You should finish the rug.**
THE BOY. And if the Christians hang us?
THE GIRL. They won't hang us. They will look at the rug and say, as they always do, what a weave you put in your rugs!
THE BOY. They will tip you on your front and pull up your skirt, on the rug or off it!
THE GIRL. How can I weave if he says that! **How can I weave!**
THE MAN. You have lost a row of stitches.
THE BOY. **And you they'll disembowel for Jesus!**
THE MAN. And another row. We are allowing the winds of passing

struggles to break our family down. Look, I still work, my fingers are as rapid as ever, or as slow as ever, but I persist, I have not dropped one stitch for fear or history.
THE GIRL. I will make up my lost row.
THE MAN. She knows! She knows all pain will be smothered in the rug. The rug is the rug my father taught me, and his taught him, back to the beginning. All Christians, and all Tartars, and all Kurds, and neither Genghis nor the Tsar have changed its features. In you, boy thirsting for a rifle, the people live, you see the message in the threads.
THE BOY. I know.
THE MAN. You say you know but you still prefer the rifle.
THE BOY. Because without the rifle there's no rug! I don't know why, but the rug and rifle are the same.

A shell falls near. THE WOMAN *rises to her feet, shocked, and lets out a cry which does not distract* THE MAN.

THE WOMAN. Don't stop — don't take any notice of me — *(Another shell. She screeches again).* It's all right, you carry on, I —
THE GIRL. Just sit. If you stand you will be hit by flying splinters.
THE BOY. A horse is hit! *(A flood of blood swiftly spreads across the stage).*
THE MAN. Perhaps the siege is nearly over. Then we shall eat again, but to eat costs money, and we shall have nothing to trade if we do not have stock. Stock is all. Stock is life.
THE GIRL. My fingers go more quickly when I think of food!
THE WOMAN. Forgive me, my nerves threaten us all. Forgive me and my nerves ...
THE GIRL. We understand, you aren't as young as you were.
THE WOMAN. I was always delicate ...
THE MAN. But your fingers worked like ants! Impeccable, relentless fingers which I saw and admired —
THE WOMAN. I was the fastest in the city!
THE MAN. She was, and I did not hesitate, I said, this woman must be my wife ...!
THE WOMAN. It is only shells that spoil my concentration. *(A shell falls near).*
THE BOY. **A man is dead in the garden!** *(A flood of blood swiftly spreads over the stage).* I should take his place ...!
THE MAN. If you abandon the fringes we will never do the rug —
THE BOY. The Christians will take the city!
THE MAN. They have taken it before.
THE BOY. That is the attitude, if I might say, the very attitude that allows them back. I do not criticize, I am doing the fringes.
THE MAN. More wool. You see, I am through my skein. More wool. *(*THE GIRL *gets up to fetch wool).* I admit, this assault has unsettled even me, or I should have had it by me. *(*THE GIRL *returns with a skein. A shell explodes. She slips in the blood and falls).*

THE BOY. Are you all right?
THE GIRL. I'm all right! Don't stop working, I'm all right. But I have fallen in the horse's blood.
THE BOY. Or the man's blood, is it?
THE GIRL. Don't stand up! The flying splinters ...! *(She crawls to them).* I'm sorry, I slipped.
THE MAN. We are working to eat. We are weaving not only for the rug, but for what the rug will buy us. Give me the wool.
THE GIRL. I'm sorry, the wool is ruined. When I slipped it fell in the horse's blood.
THE BOY. The man's blood, surely?
THE GIRL. I must go back.
THE WOMAN. Mind the flying splinters!
THE MAN. Show me ... *(Pause)* Look, the colour! The wool was pale, but the paleness has been coloured by the blood ...
THE GIRL. I'll fetch another —
THE MAN. Wait. Look, as soon as this is dry, we shall have a different red. I feel certain this is a different red.
THE GIRL. Bring more, shall I?
THE MAN. Bring more, and soak it in the blood!
THE BOY. But it's man's blood!
THE MAN. Yes ... So when this is gone, run to the hospital!
THE GIRL. The hospital?
THE MAN. Ask to take a bucket from the wounds —
THE BOY. The wounds?
THE MAN. From those who haemorrhage! You see, it has a tone which is not the same as ox's blood.
THE WOMAN. It is a beautiful and unusual red ...
THE MAN. And it will bring us customers. They will gasp and say no other weaver has such reds!
THE BOY. But that is —
THE MAN. **You quarrel with a gift from God.** You quibble at his miracles. Go, if you want, and be shot by the Christians. Die in the trenches and let their cannons grind your face —
THE WOMAN. Shh, shh —
THE MAN. I tell you, in the great cities of the world, they will bid and bicker for this stock ...
THE BOY. It is not even Christian blood ...
THE MAN. Would that improve its colour?
THE GIRL. My brother does not know how to take a gift ...
THE BOY. I do, but —
THE MAN. It will end, this war, because they always do, and then we shall have no more of this colour.
THE BOY. Cut a throat, why don't you?
THE MAN. **What use are you with your indignations and your lip all out at me?** You have not done a stitch.
THE WOMAN. The guns have stopped ...
THE BOY. The crescent flag is coming down ...!

THE MAN. Needle, quick ...
THE WOMAN. The guns have stopped ...
THE BOY. We've lost!
THE MAN. Some have.
THE GIRL. The Christians, will they give us bread?
THE WOMAN. Give? Give bread? Their own soldiers are half-starving.
THE MAN *(to* THE BOY*)*. Hurry, to the hospital! *(He goes out. Pause. The weavers work.* TWO SOLDIERS *appear. They stare at the weavers).*
FIRST SOLDIER. We took the city. And we found our soldiers crucified. Some with no eyes. Some castrated and with their pieces in their mouths.
SECOND SOLDIER. So now all bestiality is okay. All looting. And all opening of girls also okay.
FIRST SOLDIER. I'll take that rug. *(*THE MAN *grasps it defensively).*
SECOND SOLDIER. Don't be an idiot.
THE MAN. My stock!
SECOND SOLDIER. What's that? An insult in his lingo? Oi! *(He proceeds to stab* THE MAN, *who dies.* THE WOMEN *watch transfixed).*
FIRST SOLDIER *(to* THE GIRL*)*. You — with me — I am looking for a servant to wash my things — etcetera — *(*THE GIRL *gets up.* THE SECOND SOLDIER *rolls up the rug).* Don't look so scared. I am relatively kind, which is more than you lot manage ... *(They go off.* THE WOMAN *tries to scream, but is dumb and only her mouth opens.* THE BOY *returns with the bucket, looks).*
THE BOY. The rug ... *(He looks).* **The rug!**

KISS MY HANDS

CHARACTERS

WOMAN
VOICE
FIRST TERRORIST
SECOND TERRORIST
THIRD TERRORIST
HUSBAND
CHILD

A knocking on a door at night, repeated. A WOMAN *in night clothes appears from a room.*

WOMAN. We never open the door at night!
VOICE. We have been ambushed and a friend is shot!
WOMAN. Ambushed by whom?
VOICE. The terrorists!
WOMAN. Which terrorists?
VOICE. Trust us!
WOMAN. How can I?
VOICE. Because you are a human being and not a dog.
WOMAN. I am not a dog, but you might be.
VOICE. Then we have to find another house and our friend will die ... !
WOMAN. All right.
VOICE. God praise your humanity!
WOMAN. I hope so. *(She unbolts the door.* TERRORISTS *burst in).*
FIRST TERRORIST. Where is he!
SECOND TERRORIST. Bedrooms!
THIRD TERRORIST. Kitchen!
WOMAN. Oh, Christ make me deaf and you speechless ever more, you have murdered every decent impulse, you have killed all language, you are the terrorists!
FIRST TERRORIST. We are, and it's a pity to have to work this way but your husband and his ilk must be cut out of our lives like warts, and then we shall bring back good neighbours, then you'll need no bolts I promise you! *(*THE TERRORISTS *drag her* HUSBAND *in, naked and roped).*
HUSBAND. You let them in ....
WOMAN. Forgive me, I only
HUSBAND. You helped our enemies to murder me ...
WOMAN. I was not — I had not killed the instinct of a neighbour — I apologize —
HUSBAND. Now I will die because you were so ordinary ...
WOMAN. Let him go. You cheated me!
SECOND TERRORIST. One day, all normal again, and when the door is knocked on, open it ...
WOMAN. **Never open a door again.**
THIRD TERRORIST. But then the genuine will suffer
FIRST TERRORIST. Take him to the wood and shoot him there.
WOMAN. **Never open a door again.**

HUSBAND. You have made me hate my wife ... in my last minutes, feel terrible anger for my wife ...
SECOND TERRORIST. Good. You should suffer everything for your sins. I hope your child spits on your grave.
FIRST TERRORIST. When we have gone, shut the door.
WOMAN. Leave us alone ... give us a minute on our own ...
FIRST TERRORIST. If we did that, you would deceive us.
WOMAN. I swear not.
FIRST TERRORIST. How can I believe your oath? Because we cruelly cheated you, you would be justified in betraying us. This struggle wrecks the old relations! Outside with him.
WOMAN. Forgive me!
HUSBAND. I want to — I want to, but — I am dying for your error! And I had such work to do, who will replace me in the village? I might have served so many, and I perish for your error ...
SECOND TERRORIST. I love this. I had never reckoned this.
WOMAN. Struggle! Struggle to forgive!
HUSBAND. **I want to!**
WOMAN. Struggle, then ...
HUSBAND. Don't move me yet! *(They stare at him)*. To survive, we must learn everything we had forgotten, and unlearn everything we were taught, and being inhuman, overcome inhumanity. Now, kiss my hands ... *(He holds out his roped hands. She kisses them)*. All's well between us, then ... *(They take him out. She is still, then she kneels on the floor, in a ball. Pause. A child's voice)*.
CHILD'S VOICE. Mummy ... *(Pause.* THE CHILD *enters)*. What was that noise? (THE WOMAN *stares at* THE CHILD).
WOMAN. Killers.
CHILD. Mummy, don't be —
WOMAN. Fetch the pillow from your bed. *(He goes off, returns with the pillow)*. Give me the pillow. *(He gives her the pillow. She puts it over his face. He struggles. They grapple, as if endlessly. Suddenly she casts away the pillow and takes him in her arms)*. I will open the door ... **I will open the door ...!**

*THE NECESSITY FOR
PROSTITUTION IN ADVANCED
SOCIETIES*

CHARACTERS

THE OLD WOMAN
THE YOUNG WOMAN
THE YOUNG MAN

AN OLD WOMAN *in a chair.* A YOUNG WOMAN *dressing.*

THE OLD WOMAN. I thought, treading through the broken glass of rich men's houses, how simple this is ...! Picking through the bonfires of their letters and waving their corsetry on sticks, how simple, why has it never happened before ...! And standing in the soft rain of burning records from the police house, how clean, how swift ...! And then I saw, hurrying from the back door, our men, struggling with cardboard boxes, rescuing the police files from the flames, and it came vaguely to me, this would perhaps be less swift after all ...
THE YOUNG WOMAN. Don't tell me what I never lived through.
THE OLD WOMAN. I have to tell! Why don't you want to know?
THE YOUNG WOMAN. In all the books, the same old thing. In all the films, the same old thing.
THE OLD WOMAN. We have to tell!
THE YOUNG WOMAN. The heroes and the heroines. The red sashes and the rifles waving in the air.
THE OLD WOMAN. It was like that!
THE YOUNG WOMAN. The grinning face of the dirty worker. Grinning and grinning.
THE OLD WOMAN. And you, with your stockings, tugging at the seams. And your heels, you cannot sit without pointing your heels!
THE YOUNG WOMAN. I don't ask you to admire my legs. The party executives do that.
THE OLD WOMAN. You would travel half Europe for your underwear!
THE YOUNG WOMAN. The party chiefs complain if in the bedroom I am dated by my clothes. They say, don't I deserve the best dressed whores? Am I not a son of the people? You should hear! They talk of fifty years of struggle, and putting their noses to my groin they mutter how my pants redeem all sacrifice ... *(Pause).* Something like that. I am a graduate and I make it witty.
THE OLD WOMAN. We were happy. Happier than you ...
THE YOUNG WOMAN. No, I am happier because I don't believe.
THE OLD WOMAN. It is happiness to believe!
THE YOUNG WOMAN. You must justify your life. Your terrible life.
THE OLD WOMAN. Mistakes were made —
THE YOUNG WOMAN. **Errors.**
THE OLD WOMAN. *(Pause).* You call them errors, I —
THE YOUNG WOMAN. **The word is errors. Errors is the word.** *(Pause).*

I'm sorry. *(Pause)*. Shouting at an old woman. Sorry. The young are vile. But I watched the General Secretary on the television and he said, it is a sign of our greatness that we apologize to the people. These are our errors, the people must judge. What errors, too! **The bigger the error the more we must forgive.** Excellent. Sometimes I think the spirits of the executed gather round my bed and whisper as I fornicate, how miniature your errors are, your little errors barely leave a stain! *(Pause)*. Of course, I am jealous of you also. Jealous of your passions. But I hate you for being alive. You should have perished with the others. By your constant alterations you avoided the bullet. You wallow in error.

THE OLD WOMAN. History advances, not as I believed at your age, in straight lines, but in —

THE YOUNG WOMAN. **Zigzags like the seam of a falling stocking.** *(Pause)*. I am dining with a foreign diplomat. I, the daughter of the revolution, lend my body to the corrupt. He will be half-inebriated from the casino and may not penetrate. **Thus our purity may yet be saved.** *(Pause)*. I might have been the director of an enterprise, but I saw the whores waiting for the foreigners and my pity ran out to them and I wanted to know their happiness ...

THE OLD WOMAN. Happiness ...?

THE YOUNG WOMAN. It must be happiness! If it is not happiness, why should the daughters of a free society submit? It is happiness, or there has been another error.

THE OLD WOMAN. I don't know...

THE YOUNG WOMAN. You don't know ... *(She finishes her dressing)*. How beautiful I am. My teeth. My skin. The revolution has manufactured perfect girls. *(She goes out. THE OLD WOMAN stares. A YOUNG MAN enters)*.

THE YOUNG MAN. Is Magda here? Are you — Is Magda here? Gone to the brothel? Why do you —

THE OLD WOMAN. She hurt me ...

THE YOUNG MAN. Yes, she is a bitch, and with a tongue that — well, she has a tongue to lap a man to ecstasy and lash a woman into shame! She does. I admire Magda, I love Magda, but she is a bitch.

THE OLD WOMAN. I won't be —

THE YOUNG MAN. No —

THE OLD WOMAN. Made to —

THE YOUNG MAN. The young are vile, we are so vile!

THE OLD WOMAN. **Apologize for my life!**

THE YOUNG MAN. Indeed!

THE OLD WOMAN. No!

THE YOUNG MAN. History doesn't advance in straight lines, but —

THE OLD WOMAN. Who told you that?

THE YOUNG MAN. Well —

THE OLD WOMAN. Who told you that?

THE YOUNG MAN. Everybody knows that —

THE OLD WOMAN. Everybody?

THE YOUNG MAN. It's in all the schoolbooks. Have a brandy and —

THE OLD WOMAN. No!
THE YOUNG MAN. All right, don't have a brandy, I wasn't stopping anyway.
THE OLD WOMAN. How can she — how can she choose to —
THE YOUNG MAN. It's honest work —
THE OLD WOMAN. Neither work nor honest —
THE YOUNG MAN. It is work. Service for reward. That's work.
THE OLD WOMAN. But the body ...! How I wanted to say to her, except she frightens me, how I wanted to say — the body!
THE YOUNG MAN. The labourer also has a body.
THE OLD WOMAN. **Yes, but the act of love!** *(She stares at him).* I think I half went to the barricades for love. I think I threw grenades for genuine desire. And once I cut a policeman's throat for it, when he might have known desire more than me ...
THE YOUNG MAN. She knows desire. When she does it with me, then it's desire. You make an icon of her fundament, rather as her clients do. Is this the rationalism of the party?
THE OLD WOMAN. You have no souls!
THE YOUNG MAN. **I have a soul!**
THE OLD WOMAN. You murder love, then!
THE YOUNG MAN. **We murder love?** *(Pause).* You, with your eliminations and your liquidations, your rationalisations and your proscriptions, your prohibitions, your revocations, your knifing of the old and slicing of the mystical, your hacking of the incompatible and choking of the incomprehensible, the slaughter of the unnecessary, the suffocation of prejudice and the notional, the extirpation of the ideal and the fanciful, the terrible scorching of all dissonance, and you say you did it in the name of desire, you talk of souls and love — the mystical of the mystical — **To the cellars with this ancient bitch and one shot in the neck** ...! *(A gulf of silence separates them).* Forgive me, you insulted my girl friend. Or it seemed so, anyway. *(Pause).* Forgive me. The young are vile. *(He hesitates, goes out.* THE OLD WOMAN *is still. She gets up at last, and bending, picks up the discarded garments* THE YOUNG WOMAN *left. She shakes them out, puts them on hangers).*

REASONS FOR THE FALL OF EMPERORS

CHARACTERS

ALEXANDER
OFFICER
GROOM

The Emperor ALEXANDER *in his tent at night. A camp bed. An* OFFICER *in attendance. Terrible sounds distantly at intervals.*

ALEXANDER. Listen, the enemy are cutting my soldiers' throats.
OFFICER. It's wolves.
ALEXANDER. No, the enemy are cutting my soldiers' throats.
OFFICER. *(Pause).* Yes, they are. Go to bed, now.
ALEXANDER. I must listen.
OFFICER. Why?
ALEXANDER. I must.
OFFICER. *(Pause).* They do that. They will not collect the wounded. They are not like us.
ALEXANDER. I watched the battle. You were with me. Did I tremble?
OFFICER. No, not so very —
ALEXANDER. Not tremble?
OFFICER. You trembled, but not —
ALEXANDER. With fear?
OFFICER. Not with fear, no. Pity, rather, and at one point you seemed to have gone deaf.
ALEXANDER. I heard everything.
OFFICER. At one point you kicked the brandy over, a little wave over the generals' feet, and the brandy glasses rolled across the wooden deck of the observation point, splintering as they dropped ... go to bed now ... tomorrow they will begin a new attack ...
ALEXANDER. They die willingly ...
OFFICER. Yes, they shout your name.
ALEXANDER. They shout it, and they die. I heard them, shouting and dying **I cannot stand that sound** can't we send out patrols?
OFFICER. No, it is too near their lines.
ALEXANDER. It is a terrible sound.
OFFICER. They plead.
ALEXANDER. It is the worst sound in the world.
OFFICER. They plead, but still the enemy cut their throats, such is their hatred for us. I can fetch some wax for your ears.
ALEXANDER. No.
OFFICER. The officers have distributed wax to the sentries. But there is not enough for all the troops. In any case there is some disagreement as to the virtue of this wax. On the one hand it may enrage our soldiers to

hear this torture of their comrades, which is good. On the other, it may make their blood run cold and tomorrow they may falter. We have sent to the capital for more wax, but the roads are bad.

ALEXANDER. Leave me now.

OFFICER. As you wish. But if I may advise you, sleep, so you look refreshed and then the troops will think, how confident the emperor is, we must win! Whereas if you seemed tired or full of grief, they will attack despondently.

ALEXANDER. So it is in their interest I do not listen to their cries?

OFFICER. Yes. Are you sure you won't have the wax?

ALEXANDER. Good night. *(The* OFFICER *withdraws. The* EMPEROR *lies down. The sound of a boot brush, incessantly. Suddenly he sits up).* Who's there! *(Pause).* Come in, who's there! *(Pause). A* PEASANT *enters, holding the Emperor's boots).*

GROOM. Excellency?

ALEXANDER. Who are you?

GROOM. I am a groom. I am polishing the Emperor's boots. If the sound of the brushes offends him I will go behind the horse lines, perhaps he will not hear it there, but you can't be sure.

ALEXANDER. You are a peasant?

GROOM. I am. Doing six years' service with the regiment.

ALEXANDER. How does a peasant sleep?

GROOM. He sleeps better than the Emperor.

ALEXANDER. Why, do the sounds of his brothers dying not disturb his rest?

GROOM. They were born in pain. They slit the throats of oxen. They beat and sometimes kill their wives. They die of famine in filthy huts and fall into machinery. The Turk is swift with the knife, though not as swift as the Bulgarian. As for the cry, it's brief. The ox protests as well. Who hears him?

ALEXANDER. I think of this. I think of the grief in distant villages, the orphans who scour the long white lane ...

GROOM. They say the Emperor is a sensitive man. Some say they've seen him weep in hospitals.

ALEXANDER. He does.

GROOM. But the war must go on, at least until it stops.

ALEXANDER. *(Pause).* When I hear you, little brother, I know I must build more schools. Do you read?

GROOM. Read what?

ALEXANDER. The Bible.

GROOM. No, but I listen, and agree with every word of it.

ALEXANDER. Is it not often contradictory?

GROOM. I agree with all the contradictions, too. As for schools, if I could read the gentlemen's books, I should only lose sleep, and then the battle would certainly be lost and the Turks would slit not only our throats but the Emperor's too, and that would surely be the end of the world.

ALEXANDER. Do you love the Emperor?

GROOM. It is impossible not to love him!

ALEXANDER. But he weeps so much!

GROOM. I forgive him for that. I had an aunt who wept continually but could not say why. She just wept.

ALEXANDER. He weeps for you.

GROOM. And we for him! We do! Shall I get on with the boots? He will need them in the morning. *(He goes to pick them up).*

ALEXANDER. **I think that's wrong.**

GROOM. *(Stopping).* I apologize to His Excellency. I am a boot polisher and unable to follow arguments —

ALEXANDER. **Liar.**

GROOM. I am sure we all lie but only by accident —

ALEXANDER. **You are not so wooden as —**

GROOM. No, obviously not —

ALEXANDER. **As you pretend.** *(Pause. They stare at one another).* Oh, little brother, I could kiss you on the mouth ...

GROOM. My mouth, as all my flesh, is at Your Excellency's service ... *(The EMPEROR sits on the bed and weeps silently. The GROOM watches. Pause).* My brother died today. So when I get home I shall have twice as many children. Life ... ! He was a good father and drank so much he punched their eyes black, one after another! Still, they'll weep! And if I die ... !

ALEXANDER. Don't go on ...

GROOM. Then it's the orphanage, but the orphanages are chock-a-block after this war, so they'll end up roaming and probably criminals —

ALEXANDER. Don't go on ...

GROOM. There's a murderer in all of us, God says so, so a couple will be hanged and a couple flogged, and a stranger hacked to pieces in his drawing room, but then the war has little wars inside it like one of His Excellency's decorated eggs —

ALEXANDER. **I said I —**

GROOM. I only meant — it is not good for an emperor to weep in front of a peasant.

ALEXANDER. On the contrary, what is your love worth if it attaches itself only to a dummy? **That sound!**

GROOM. It is a good sound, believe me! It is the sound of sacrifice, you should hear it as another hymn to your house, different in tone but not in quality, from the crowd's gasp at your coronation. The Emperor should know the people will go on dying until the villages are dry sticks and the cattle skeletons. The dead only encourage further sacrifice. Along a road of skulls he might dance if he chose to ... !

ALEXANDER. *(Pause).* I will put an end to slavery. I will abolish feudalism. I will place teachers in every hamlet. I will break the stooping habit and the ingrained servility of serfs. I will run electricity to every hut and create a corps of critics who will yell at every inhumanity!

GROOM. *(Pause).* I must finish the boots. It will be dawn and they need all hands at the batteries.

ALEXANDER. Undress me *(Pause. The GROOM puts down the boots. He goes to the EMPEROR and unbuttons his tunic. He removes it).* Your fingers do not tremble ...

GROOM. Why should they? If they trembled it could only be because I was disloyal or entertained some thought of treason, or even that I felt my position shameful in some way, which I do not. How much clothing should I remove?

ALEXANDER. The emperor will be naked.

GROOM. He will be cold. *(A cry in the distance).*

ALEXANDER. Then it will be him who trembles. *(The GROOM proceeds).* Oh, there is shit in my pants!

GROOM. Yes. Has His Excellency a chill on the bowel?

ALEXANDER. He was seized by terror during the attack ...

GROOM. It was a terrible battle. Our soldiers climbed each other to the Turkish trench.

ALEXANDER. I wept, and I shat ...

GROOM. *(Folding the clothes).* The error was the lack of high explosive shell. The trenches were undamaged.

ALEXANDER. And I pleaded, blow the retreat!

GROOM. Yes, I heard the bugle! Which was I think, unfortunate, because the retreating men collided with the second wave and more died in the confusion than if the attack had been pressed —

ALEXANDER. That was me — and only me —

GROOM. It is the Emperor's right to have bugles blown at his whim —

ALEXANDER. They died, and yet more died ...

GROOM. Better luck tomorrow. Shall you keep your socks on? The earth is damp.

ALEXANDER. **No socks.**

GROOM. The Emperor is goose-fleshed, shall I massage his limb?

ALEXANDER. **No massage.** *(He stands naked, shivering. A distant cry).* You are dressed and I am naked. You are strong and I am weak. You are fine and I am stunted.

GROOM. Yes.

ALEXANDER. Justify your failure to assassinate me, then.

GROOM. Justify ... ?

ALEXANDER. Yes, justify it.

GROOM. The Emperor takes me for a wolf. I am offended he should think I am a wolf. But let him offend where he wishes. He is the Emperor. *(A Pause. ALEXANDER looks into him. Suddenly he shouts).*

ALEXANDER. **Flog this man! Hey! Flog this man!** *(The OFFICER enters).*

GROOM. What for ... ?

ALEXANDER. **Flog and flog this man!**

GROOM. In Jesus' name, what for ... ? *(The OFFICER takes the man by the shoulder).*

ALEXANDER. What for? No reason. Flog him for no reason. *(He is taken out. ALEXANDER sits. A cry in the distance. The OFFICER enters).*

OFFICER. You want him flogged? You're sure?

ALEXANDER. Yes. And do it now. *(The OFFICER goes out. Pause. A cry in the distance. He stands. The sound of flogging begins, monotonous.*

ALEXANDER *Listens. A cry in the distance).* **The boots!** *(The* OFFICER *enters).* No one is buffing the boots. *(The* OFFICER *picks up the boots, goes out. To the other sounds, the brushing of boots.* ALEXANDER *stares into the dark. He is engulfed by sound, the sound fills him).*

ONLY SOME CAN TAKE THE STRAIN

CHARACTERS

**BOOKSELLER
THE MAN
THE WOMAN**

An AGEING MAN *appears with a handcart. The handcart is laden with books.*

BOOKSELLER. Usual wind on the embankment. Usual unkind wind. *(Pause)*. Usual bird shit on the volumes. Usual unkind birds. *(Pause. He wipes the books)*. I railed at the birds. I railed at the wind. But I was young, then. Now I say, shit on! Blow on! *(Pause)*. Usual fumes from the motor cars. The ever-increasing torrent of motor cars. Our arteries are clogged with anxiety, our lungs are corroded with fumes. **What a conspiracy and nobody knows except me.** We are out of control, oh, so out of control. *(He shuffles the books)*. Yesterday I sold a book. To be precise, I took money and surrendered a book. This was certainly what is commonly known as a sale. Unfortunately, or fortunately, since not every setback appears so on reflection, hardly had the customer left the stall when for some obscure reason I shall never understand, he turned on his heel and replacing the book, asked for his money back. I said, you do this to torture me! But thinking this over during the night, I have concluded that this peculiar action was, in the most general sense, beneficial, since I have the book still in my stock and consequently the knowledge it contains remains in safe hands. I regard it as a bookseller's mission to be cautious regarding who might get his hands on stock. *(Pause. He fusses)*. Of course this cannot last. This will not be allowed to last. **They will act.** Both I and the books will be **eliminated.** I have lived with this for years. I knew, as if by intuition, that time was short. I knew we would be burned. The books burned, and the booksellers also. You think the stake was something of the Middle Ages? No, they shall be my pyre, and I, their pyre. **Oh, something has shit on the books!** *(He pulls out a dirty cloth, rubs a volume)*. Oh, we are out of control, so out of control …! *(A figure has appeared who stares at* THE BOOKSELLER. THE BOOKSELLER *is aware)*. Police. *(He rubs on)*. I act dishevelled. I act the tramp. This way I avoid the attention of both criminals and police. This way the cart appears to be a cart of junk and not, as it is, a pantechnicon of truth which might lever up the world.
THE MAN *(tentatively)*. All right if I —
BOOKSELLER. Browse, yes, do browse. *(*THE MAN *examines the books)*. They are closing in on me. They no longer bother to disguise their intentions. I can almost, if I try, I can almost smell the charring of leaves and flesh. But though elimination awaits me with its twisted eye I struggle on.

THE MAN *(with a title)*. I have been looking for this everywhere!
BOOKSELLER. Ah.
THE MAN. Everywhere!
BOOKSELLER. You see, it exists.
THE MAN. It does, it does indeed.
BOOKSELLER. Oh, yes, it exists.
THE MAN. How much? It has no price.
BOOKSELLER. It has a price.
THE MAN. Where? *(He turns the book round).* Is that the price? Is that seriously the price?
BOOKSELLER. The price is perfectly serious, but are you?
THE MAN *(amazed)*. But that is …!
BOOKSELLER. Do you want everybody reading it?
THE MAN. But —
BOOKSELLER. Its price is merely the reflection of its power.
THE MAN. That may be so, but —
BOOKSELLER. Anyway, I don't want to let it go.
THE MAN. You don't want to sell the book?
BOOKSELLER. No.
THE MAN. But it's on the counter and it's priced —
BOOKSELLER. And you think that's evidence I wish to sell it? It proves nothing. Any day I might regret selling it, and then I should have to track you down. God knows where you might take refuge. In any case, how do I know you will understand it? It may be beyond your comprehension. The book will therefore be wasted. The efforts of the author, the printer and the publisher, all wasted. Criminal. No, I have to be sure.
THE MAN. I can't find this book anywhere. I must have it, even though the price is —
BOOKSELLER. Not absurd —
THE MAN. Not absurd, perhaps —
BOOKSELLER. No, in fact, given its scarcity and my reluctance to sell, it is oddly cheap.
THE MAN. Given that you don't want to sell —
BOOKSELLER. It is dirt cheap **and you are the police.**
THE MAN *(pause)*. I am the police?
BOOKSELLER. Yes. And that explains your hunger for the title. Only the police show such persistence in the tracking down of literature.
THE MAN. I assure you I —
BOOKSELLER. Never mind your assurances —
THE MAN. I wanted the book —
BOOKSELLER. To burn. And then, late in the night, you will return to burn me. I shan't be here, however. I shall be on the road. I shan't say which. And those who want the truth will say, he's not here today, he's on the road. We must tramp the streets of every city. Probably he is in Zurich.
THE MAN. Listen, I am honourable and want the knowledge I believe this title might contain.
BOOKSELLER. Or Frankfurt. He is in Frankfurt, they will say. *(*THE

MAN *shakes his head, starts to move off).* Damn all oppressors! *(*THE MAN *goes).* I hate to swear but I think, to fend off his type, it is permitted occasionally to swear. **Shit! The pigeon also hates my trade!** *(He wipes the counter with a filthy cloth).* Understandable. Look how populous and base the pigeon is. The more it shits the more certain I become that I am the last disseminator of knowledge. No doubt the oppressor is returning to his station to collect a squad. This squad will beat me to death here on the embankment, and no one will look. And he pretended, most convincingly, to want the book. *(He polishes it).* I have had this by me twenty years. I have saved it from unscrupulous buyers at least five times. It is a struggle, a terrible struggle not to sell and I am tired. I honestly believe he would have paid **three times the price.** That is the measure of how unscrupulous he was. How long can I keep this up? This lonely life? In certain states of light I smell my pyre ... *(*A WOMAN *appears).* I am shutting. I have been open long enough today. *(He starts to pull the canvas over).*

THE WOMAN. Are you the bookseller?

BOOKSELLER. No.

THE WOMAN. Then what's —

BOOKSELLER. Beetroot.

THE WOMAN. Then why aren't your hands red?

BOOKSELLER. You know everything. Why are you pestering me? I am an old man and they have wanted to eliminate me all these years. God alone knows how I have evaded them.

THE WOMAN. I will help you.

BOOKSELLER. Help?

THE WOMAN. Yes.

BOOKSELLER. Help how, exactly? I need no help. You are a murderer. It is a well-known characteristic of murderers to offer help. I have a whistle here which I will blow until the last breath leaves my body. And though they will not stir from their cars but only watch me through the windows still I will whistle.

THE WOMAN. Your lonely struggle ...

BOOKSELLER. I have been married, thank you.

THE WOMAN. Your imminent death ...

BOOKSELLER. What is this? Death is always imminent. It was imminent when I first lay screaming in the scales. Are you a philosopher? Not a very good philosopher and thank you I have been married.

THE WOMAN. The truth ...

BOOKSELLER. What do you know about the truth?

THE WOMAN. In the cart.

BOOKSELLER. I have to go. I am meeting a man who runs a theatre.

THE WOMAN. And what have you ever done for the common man?

BOOKSELLER. I have never seen one. Now if you will be so —

THE WOMAN. I am impounding the books. I am Miss Leishman from the Ministry of Education.

BOOKSELLER. There's no such thing

THE WOMAN. Put down the handles of your cart, I am officially sealing

your stock. *(She takes a roll of sticky tape from her bag).*
BOOKSELLER. I was expecting you! All these years I was expecting you!
THE WOMAN. This is an Official Seal. *(She winds it round the cart).*
BOOKSELLER. **My speech from the pyre!**
THE WOMAN. Later, someone will give you an inventory.
BOOKSELLER. The cars go by! The truth is sealed and the cars go by!
THE WOMAN. And the pigeons shit.
BOOKSELLER. They would do, nothing stops their cloaca. I once saw pigeons shit on a tramp as she gave birth, and the fall of the Bastille did not change their habits.
THE WOMAN. There, sealed up ...
BOOKSELLER. **Never to see the light again.**
THE WOMAN. Policies change. Yesterday's shocker is tomorrow's standard text.
BOOKSELLER. More philosophy, where are you trained?
THE WOMAN. You are not to break the seals, all right?
BOOKSELLER. I am tired and I ache for the stake ...
THE WOMAN. A van will be along —
BOOKSELLER. Driven by them ...
THE WOMAN. By Brian and Gary, I expect ... *(She leaves).*
BOOKSELLER. They hunted us, and with such human expression. We are out of control when the oppressor has a human face, so out of control ...
THE MAN *appears again.*
THE MAN. Your rudeness almost dissuaded me. I walked four streets and then I thought, I need the knowledge, why be put off? Knowledge only comes to the one who perseveres. I also called at the bank.
BOOKSELLER. Too late.
THE MAN. **It's sold?**
BOOKSELLER. Not sold, but too late.
THE MAN. You are maddeningly obscure and I will have the book if I have to fight you for it. Take your glasses off.
BOOKSELLER. The seals of the State are on my stock.
THE MAN *(pause).* Idiot.
BOOKSELLER. Idiot, yes. All my life I struggled. That is the mark of an idiot.
THE MAN. Then where is the author?
BOOKSELLER. The author? Dead, or he became a postman. I forget. Anyway, he could tell you nothing.
THE MAN. Very well. Open the box.
BOOKSELLER. **Open the box?**
THE MAN. Why ever not?
BOOKSELLER. It's gaol and I am seventy.
THE MAN. This is gaol and I am twenty.
BOOKSELLER. The van will be here.
THE MAN. But look, the traffic's heavy, they will be stuck and the engine will overheat. We have hours.
BOOKSELLER. What is this reckless thirst that masters you?
THE MAN. It is the only copy.

BOOKSELLER. How many did you want?

THE MAN. I am breaking the seals.

BOOKSELLER. You are going to disseminate it! I knew when I saw you, he is either a policeman or a disseminator! You will copy it on machines and leave the pages in launderettes.

THE MAN. Yes.

BOOKSELLER. I knew! What do you think knowledge is? Sherbert? *(THE MAN is cutting the seals with a knife).* Enticer! What are you trying to do, wreck people's lives? **Only some can take the strain!** *(THE MAN covers THE BOOKSELLER's mouth).*

THE MAN. Speak and you die. *(Pause. He frees him, finishes cutting the seals, and removes the book. He conceals it under his coat.* THE BOOKSELLER *is still.* THE MAN *turns to go).*

BOOKSELLER. Zurich. *(THE MAN stops).* Down by the river. *(THE MAN leaves).* Under the tree.

THE DUMB WOMAN'S ECSTASY

CHARACTERS

THE TORTURER
THE WOMAN
THE YOUTH

A widow's house. A MAN *arrives with a bag of tools.* THE WOMAN *is seated.*

THE TORTURER. They said if I came here you would have a room. Have you a room? *(She looks at him).* You have a room? You have a room but you don't know if you like me? Understandable. I am not local and the accent's odd. Perhaps I'm dirty from the road? I'll pay in advance. Or rather, as I have no money yet, I will give you the toolbag as a pledge. *(He puts the bag down).* They say they pay on Fridays. What do you say? I am a foreigner, but though I am in many ways unlike you, in others I am identical, so we might progress from there. *(She just looks).* I don't know what your silence means. I have come across many silent people, but in the end, they spoke. Perhaps that is how it will be with you. I am a skilled man and eat a light breakfast. Also, I sleep soundly and bring no friends back to my lodgings. I am not solitary, but neither am I convivial. What do you say? I won't plead for a room. I would rather lie in a ditch than plead. I am proud, which is perhaps my single fault. *(Pause. He picks up the bag).* All right, I haven't satisfied you. *(He starts to go, then stops).* Ah, now I remember. You are deaf and dumb! They told me at the castle, she lets rooms but she is deaf and dumb. Now I have made us both feel foolish! *(He laughs. Pause).* I am the torturer from Poland and I have been offered a post at the castle. The new lord said there could be no more torture it was against his conscience and dismissed the old one, who, like me, set off across the country in search of a new post. But after six months, the necessity for torture made itself apparent, as it always does, and execution also could not be done without for long, so it was my luck to knock at his gate when the vacancy existed and the need was obvious to all. I have references from previous employers, all of whom were sorry to see me go, but I am a wanderer, I love to travel and I know my trade is never low for long, now shall I go up you unpleasant hag I detest the sight of you and one interview in a day is quite enough. Your eye is fixed on mine like a crow on dying vermin and I know your rooms all stink. *(He picks up the bag, and goes up to his room. A* YOUTH *creeps in).*

THE YOUTH. He's here? He's taken the room? I'll wait. *(Pause).* Listen, he bangs about! He kicks the furniture! And stamping on the boards! Dust falls from the ceiling! *(Pause).* And now he dreams ... Bring him some soup! Poles love their dinner! *(THE* WOMAN *goes out.* THE TORTURER *appears).*

THE TORTURER. A stinking crevice of a room.

THE YOUTH. It is a cheap and dirty hovel for a man like you.

THE TORTURER. It is a gutter of a room, a sewer of a room which my body shrinks to lie in, and the sheet is steeped in dead men's vomit. However, I am here now.

THE YOUTH. It is a scandal that a man like you should —

THE TORTURER. Yes —

THE YOUTH. Whose skills deserve the highest respect and the appropriate accommodation.

THE TORTURER. You flatter brilliantly but I do not take apprentices. All I do I do myself.

THE YOUTH. I admire that. The single-minded craftsman who leaves behind him only —

THE TORTURER. Pain —

THE YOUTH. Or truth? Just as the cabinet maker, with his tools on his back, leaves in a string of villages the mended doors and little boxes of his craft, so you —

THE TORTURER. Burst thumbs and leave eye sockets dark as pits.

THE YOUTH. You are so clear and unambiguous, I do admire you, I have no craft —

THE TORTURER. You flatter brilliantly.

THE YOUTH. Do I?

THE TORTURER. Perhaps there is employment for you there.

THE YOUTH. As a flatterer?

THE TORTURER. Yes, have you never thought of that?

THE YOUTH. As a profession? No …

THE TORTURER. I never thought of pain, either, as a profession, yet I have never gone without food, women, or a bed. These discoveries are like lightning flashes, they can illuminate your life.

THE YOUTH. I will give it some thought. *(*THE WOMAN *enters with a bowl.* THE TORTURER *sits and eats).*

THE TORTURER. What I despise is bad workmanship.

THE YOUTH. Oh, yes!

THE TORTURER. Just as a flatterer flatters best when he half-believes his compliments, so a man in my trade must concentrate on one thing only — the confession, and not indulge in pain for pain's sake. I have sometimes achieved my ends not by the infliction of pain, but merely by the description. Punishment is another matter. Punishment I never thought of as a work for life. But others do, obviously. This soup is the very sediment of drains. Why is she dumb? Because she's deaf?

THE YOUTH. She has no tongue. And her eardrums burst.

THE TORTURER. Is that so?

THE YOUTH. She is my mother but maternity has limits to its commands, and you're right, she's dirty. I sometimes beat her, and then I think, no, she gave me birth!

THE TORTURER. So rats do their verminous offspring.

THE YOUTH. It is a silly sentiment.

THE TORTURER. Our births result from squalid fornications, we were

THE DUMB WOMAN'S ECSTASY

not thought of then.
THE YOUTH. I never thought of that! You do go — beyond the obvious.
THE TORTURER. Your compliments come naturally.
THE YOUTH. Only out of admiration!
THE TORTURER. There you go again!
THE YOUTH *(laughing)*. Oh, yes —
THE TORTURER. You cannot stop yourself!
THE YOUTH. No, no! But who would employ a flatterer?
THE TORTURER. A man in power, obviously.
THE YOUTH. Yes, a man in power.
THE TORTURER. Or alternatively, a recluse.
THE YOUTH. A recluse?
THE TORTURER. Yes, for in renouncing power, he hungers for congratulation.
THE YOUTH. We all love that ...
THE TORTURER *(pause)*. She looks at me like a beaten animal, a mongrel half-drowned, this thing you call a mother.
THE YOUTH. I don't know why she cannot be content. Her life is not so bad. She was kept in the castle for less than seven years. Some never leave. No, she is lucky but quite without gratitude.
THE TORTURER. For what offence?
THE YOUTH. Selfishness.
THE TORTURER. Is that an offence?
THE YOUTH. Oh, yes! She claimed to know things others didn't. She spoke in long sentences. *(Suddenly* THE TORTURER *gets up from the table and going to a corner of the room, he thrusts his finger down his throat and vomits)*. What — Are you — Is it — *(*THE TORTURER *makes a sign of impatience, wipes his mouth, returns to his chair)*. Can I —
THE TORTURER. It is an odd thing, that sometimes, though only in rare cases, those who have suffered lack the dignity that comes with the experience and seek petty revenge. It is possible the soup was poisoned. I don't assert it, I only say it's possible. And the way the hag looked at me, it's clear she hasn't accommodated to the grandeur of spirit pain can bestow.
THE YOUTH *(pause)*. Amazing man ...
THE TORTURER. It is easy to be amazing, simply by stating the truth. I have so few enemies, yet I have led people down terrible corridors of pain ...
THE YOUTH. For truth.
THE TORTURER. Truth? I never ask for truth. Only for confession.
THE YOUTH. I see.
THE TORTURER. Do you?
THE YOUTH. I try.
THE TORTURER. The confession, even if invalid, improves the soul. The victim participates in the act which led to his arrest and in doing so shares, on the one hand, the moral power of the crime, which may have been a crime of freedom, or on the other, the universal evil of mankind,

if the crime was only malice. There is no such thing as arbitrary punishment.

THE YOUTH. You mean we all —

THE TORTURER. Deserve our pain. I remember this when my victim cries out in despair, 'But I am innocent!' I think, if she were in the throes of illness she would not cry 'I'm innocent,' would she?

THE YOUTH *(pause)*. So torture's illness? *(Pause.* THE TORTURER *gets up).*

THE TORTURER. Does she sleep at all? She has the hollow eyes of an insomniac.

THE YOUTH. But you will one day find your own corpse on the rack!

THE TORTURER *(pause, he looks at* THE YOUTH *a long time).* I expect it daily. Of course I keep my eyes open, no man willingly exposes himself to a disease. And I frequently move on.

THE YOUTH. You have the right belief for such a craft.

THE TORTURER. I had the good fortune to be trained by a religious man, and after him, a man who had cursed God out of his life. They shared this view, however, that life and pain are inextricable. Is there an inn here? I drink deeply before bed.

THE YOUTH. I think you will find the company dull and their stench noxious, you are so fastidious in mind and body —

THE TORTURER. Remember, when you begin your new career, not to describe yourself as Flatterer, but Truth Teller. Emphasize your cruelty, the harshness of your judgements. Then carry on in your normal way. You will soon be shot of this hovel. *(He goes out.* THE WOMAN *looks at* THE YOUTH*).*

THE YOUTH. Yes. I know. I know and I will. **I said I will.** When he returns drunk, or less than drunk, I will. Go up and wait. When you hear it, come down fast, with a swab and a bucket.

THE WOMAN *withdraws.* THE YOUTH *paces uneasily, taking out a pocket knife, which he wipes and clasps again.* THE TORTURER *returns.*

THE TORTURER. You're right. It stinks and the quality of life is bestial.

THE YOUTH. Did you drink much? You were not long.

THE TORTURER. Much, yes. I find the bestial society brews the best ale.

THE YOUTH. You drank much? And yet you seem — if anything — more vigorous.

THE TORTURER. Would you want me otherwise?

THE YOUTH. Never. Merely that normally our lodgers come back on four legs from there.

THE TORTURER. Perhaps they have no work to go to in the morning.

THE YOUTH. None, most of them.

THE TORTURER. And is the hag asleep?

THE YOUTH. She's gone up.

THE TORTURER. Me, too, then, for the pissy blanket.

THE YOUTH. Good night.

THE TORTURER. Good night — *(Suddenly* THE TORTURER *turns on his heel and seizes* THE YOUTH *in a cruel embrace. He cries out. They struggle).* Dance!

THE YOUTH. What — I —

THE TORTURER. Dance! *(He spins him round in a mocking dance. A chair crashes over).*

THE YOUTH. Dance — I —

THE TORTURER. Dance! Dance with me in this —

THE YOUTH. Can't — breathe —

THE TORTURER. — This palace of — hospitality —

THE YOUTH. Can't —

THE TORTURER. Love, oh, love …!

THE YOUTH. Oh …

THE TORTURER *(crushing him).* Speak, love …! *(They spin around the floor).* Oh, speak your heart to me! *(*THE WOMAN *appears with the mop and bucket.* THE TORTURER *stops the dance, holding* THE YOUTH *fixed and half-conscious).* She comes, equipped as I do, at the end of a busy day, to swab the stains away … **I also love life.** *(Pause.* THE WOMAN *falls on her knees).* She pleads … *(Dumbly, she implores him).* Silently … How good it is … her fashion … how eloquent her silence is … *(The youth struggles).* Shh! *(He tightens his grip).* Oh, this is torture … through all her hatred she must plead with me …

THE YOUTH. She loves me …!

THE TORTURER. Yes … she offers herself …! Let me …! Let me …! Who has known pain, know more … and all this suffering's for you … it is a second birth …! *(As* THE WOMAN *acts her agony,* THE TORTURER *throttles* THE YOUTH, *and lets his body slip to the floor. He goes to the table and sits.* THE WOMAN *is still.* THE TORTURER *breathes deep).* Oh, mother … I confirm you, mother … in your deep fear … I'll be your son, now. I will dig the garden. I'll stay.

SHE SEES THE ARGUMENT BUT

CHARACTERS

THE OFFICIAL
WOMAN
MAN

A WOMAN OFFICIAL, *seated behind a desk. A* WOMAN *enters, stands before her.*

THE OFFICIAL. We are so glad you could come.
WOMAN. It was — *(She makes a gesture of casualness).*
THE OFFICIAL. So glad. *(Pause)* I can see your ankle. *(Pause)* Do you realize that? *(Pause)* You do realize, of course. *(Pause)* And your eyes are outlined in —
WOMAN. Mascara.
OFFICIAL. Mascara, yes. *(Pause)* Very glad you came because we want to understand and I think you do, too. Terribly want to understand! *(Pause)* You see, all this is, we believe, a positive encouragement to criminality. Speak if you want to. *(Pause)* We feel you aid the social enemy. You put yourself at risk, but also, others. The ankle is — your ankle in particular is — immensely stimulating, as I think you know.
WOMAN. I have good ankles.
OFFICIAL. Good? I don't know about good, do you? In what way good? In a sense they are very bad because they stimulate this feeling I am referring to.
WOMAN. I don't like boiler suits.
OFFICIAL. People call them boiler suits! The word boiler suit is meant to — isn't it — prejudice? I don't think we should have called them boiler suits in the first place. In any case we did not succeed with them. For one thing, girls tightened the seats, or undid buttons far below the needs of ventilation. So, indeed, I share your irritation with the boiler suit. But the ankle. What are you trying to do? *(Pause)* You can speak to me, you know. We only want to understand.
WOMAN. *(Pause).* I wish to — this is a difficult question —
OFFICIAL. Is it? You have drawn attention to your ankle, so presumably you must know why. *(Pause).*
WOMAN. Not really, no.
OFFICIAL. You don't know why! How bewildering! You go and buy a length of rather fine wool — many weeks of wages for a typist, I suggest — cut, alter and hem it at this specific point, showing the ankle — without knowing why. Is that honestly the case? *(Pause)* I am so glad you came in.
WOMAN. *(Pause).* I wanted men to suffer for me.
OFFICIAL. *(Pause).* Suffer?
WOMAN. Torment, yes.

OFFICIAL. *(Pause)*. I think, don't you, society is so riddled with crisis now, so much healing needs to be done? Crisis after crisis? The food crisis, the health crisis, the newspaper crisis, the suicide epidemic, the lunacy epidemic? So much despair and so much healing to be done? And you say, to all this misery I would add a little more despair, a despair of my own making because it is despair, isn't it? The effect of your ankle on the morning tram, despair?

WOMAN. Yes. Longing and despair.

OFFICIAL. Though of course, among the despairing lurks the criminal. And he, tormented as you wish, will not walk home in silence to his wife, and take his children in his arms with a slightly distant look ... No, the criminal will own. No city banker has more passion to own. Which is why we stipulated, for a while, the boiler suit. For a long time this damped the criminal statistics. Then they crept up again, thanks to the tightening of the seat and the unnecessary open buttons. You advertise your sexuality.

WOMAN. Yes.

OFFICIAL. I am so glad you came in! *(Pause)* Why don't you marry and show this ankle to your husband?

WOMAN. I am married.

OFFICIAL. You are married! Then why aren't you satisfied to show this ankle in the privacy of your own home?

WOMAN. I don't know.

OFFICIAL. Perhaps you have a secret longing to betray him?

WOMAN. I'm certain of it.

OFFICIAL. You no longer love him?

WOMAN. I love him.

OFFICIAL. You love your husband but you show your ankles to any stranger in the hope of tormenting him, is that correct?

WOMAN. I think so, yes.

OFFICIAL. And where is your responsibility towards the male who cannot contain the lust you stimulate in him?

WOMAN. He should bear his suffering.

OFFICIAL. But you impose it on him!

WOMAN. Yes, and he must bear it. Perhaps I may be seduced. A correct glance or gesture, even a sign of modesty, may do the trick.

OFFICIAL. You are a married woman and you say you may be seduced —

WOMAN. Yes, I am trying to be honest —

OFFICIAL. Bewildering honesty!

WOMAN. Well, do you want me to be honest or not? *(Pause)* I have not yet met this man. But somewhere I have no doubt he does exist.

OFFICIAL. And you are seeking him?

WOMAN. *(Pause)*. I think so, yes.

OFFICIAL. *(Pause)*. The world goes on, crises occur, we struggle towards the perfection of democracy, and you, a married woman, dangles her ankle on the bus.

WOMAN. *(Pause)*. Yes.

OFFICIAL. **You deserve every unwelcome attention that you get.**

WOMAN. Ah ...
OFFICIAL. And I must say, were some monster brought before me on a charge of violation I should say half-guilty, only half! *(Pause)* My feelings. My real feelings have — soaked through ...
WOMAN. Good.
OFFICIAL. Don't please, carry your enthusiasm for honesty to such inordinate and — *(A MAN has entered and sits at the back).*
WOMAN. Who's he ... ?
OFFICIAL. The question is, are you mad?
WOMAN. Who's he?
OFFICIAL. I am married, and I have children also, I am capable of love, and have a sexual life, but I do not display myself in public, do I? Perhaps you are mad, have you considered —
WOMAN. Who is he?
OFFICIAL. You see, you cannot see a man without —
WOMAN. I just wanted to —
OFFICIAL. The very locality of a man sets off in you some —
WOMAN. How can I continue to be honest when there is a —
OFFICIAL. **He is a human being just like us.** *(Pause).* Such is the scale of your obsession you refuse to believe he can observe you simply as a person. You think, my ankle will prevent him being a **person** and force him to be a **man**. You continually subvert his right to be a simple person, you **oppress him**. *(Pause)*. But he refuses you. He is free. How peaceful he is. He observes you with a wonderful and objective comradeship. Your ankle is simply an exposed and consequently, somewhat absurd, piece of human flesh. Does he show you his? He also has an ankle.
WOMAN. *(Pause).* You are trying to wreck our sanity.
OFFICIAL. Oh, listen, if rational argument is going to be construed as an attempt on your sanity, then your sanity has to be doubted. Is it wrecking your sanity if a man does not suffer your sex?
WOMAN. Perhaps.
OFFICIAL. You define yourself by sexuality?
WOMAN. Yes —
OFFICIAL. You admit your slavery to some arbitrary gendering?
WOMAN. Yes —
OFFICIAL. Bewildering!
WOMAN. I think — this man — this person — frightens me more than a violator would —
OFFICIAL. Oh!
WOMAN. **I am trying to be honest.**
OFFICIAL. **Well, that's not enough!** *(Pause).* That's merely an indulgence. You want us to admire you. But we think you are possibly mad.
WOMAN. *(Pause).* I have to go.
OFFICIAL. The question is, have we the resources to provide a police force whose time and energy are consumed in searching for the violator of women like you? After all, there is a crisis. *(Pause).* (THE WOMAN *goes to* THE MAN).

WOMAN. You must try to save yourself.
OFFICIAL. Ha!
WOMAN. Yes, you have to try —
OFFICIAL. You look an idiot in those heels —
WOMAN. Look — look at me —
OFFICIAL. He is not moved — he merely suffers the embarrassment any man feels in the presence of a woman who is mad —
WOMAN. Look at me — *(She slaps him around the face).*
THE MAN. She hit me! *(Pause.* THE WOMAN *goes to the table, leans on it).*
WOMAN. You want me to be mad, when it is you who is mad.
OFFICIAL. Am I wearing funny heels? Is my clothing so tight I cannot move naturally? Find a mirror, look in it, and ask yourself who's mad. Look in your eyes, which are ringed with soot, and ask yourself who's mad?
WOMAN. *(Pause.* THE WOMAN *is still).* You make me ashamed ... of things I should not be ashamed of ...
OFFICIAL. We only want to understand ... (Pause. THE WOMAN *leaves the table, goes out. The sound of her heels descending stone stairs).*

THE UNFORESEEN CONSEQUENCES OF A PATRIOTIC ACT

CHARACTERS

JUDITH
THE SERVANT
THE WOMAN

JUDITH, *a year after the slaying of Holofernes, has returned to the country.*

JUDITH. The Israelites could not overcome their enemy, whose resourcefulness was greater than their power. So they sent me to seduce him, being the most beautiful woman of the time, and simple. I went with a servant to his camp, and seduced him. And while he slept, I cut off his head.

THE SERVANT. We put the head in a bag. We carried it past the sentries. What's in the bag, they said. The future of Israel, we replied. A week later Judith lost the power of speech.

JUDITH. For eight months I was dumb.

THE SERVANT. What a blow this was! Because she was the heroine of Israel and looked so sick. What use is a sick hero? So they sent her to the country, and there she gave birth. And with the child, came speech.

A WOMAN FROM THE CITY enters.

THE WOMAN. How happy you seem here...!

THE SERVANT. She is!

THE WOMAN. How happy, but no one can place their happiness above all things. Sadly. No one.

THE SERVANT. Why not?

THE WOMAN. Judith, what an example you have set to women everywhere. And on every front our armies drive the enemy beyond the frontier! New frontiers now!

THE SERVANT. And new enemies.

THE WOMAN. None of this was possible but for you. Come back to the city.

JUDITH. I love the quiet.

THE WOMAN. Yes, but just as you owed service to your people, so your people must be allowed to express its gratitude to you!

THE SERVANT. Too bad.

THE WOMAN. It does seem churlish, this exile, this lingering. It curdles the pride they feel in victory. And bring the child! We can accommodate the child. Through the child we show we might be reconciled even with Holofernes's tribes.

THE SERVANT. We haven't packed the olives.

THE WOMAN. Judith, I appeal to you in the name of the people!

THE SERVANT. Oh, don't do that —
THE WOMAN. **Must this person be allowed to speak!** *(Pause)*. I'm sorry. I spit. I froth. Forgive me.
JUDITH. I have done enough for the people.
THE WOMAN. Can anyone?
JUDITH. Yes, I have. I have done too much.
THE WOMAN. You made a sacrifice, perhaps the greatest sacrifice a woman can —
JUDITH. I think so, too —
THE WOMAN. To sleep with a man against your will, and you are ashamed —
JUDITH. Oh, no —
THE WOMAN. You feel humiliated and —
JUDITH. No. I often slept with men I did not love, often, I assure you, and never felt ashamed.
THE WOMAN *(pause)*. That is as maybe.
JUDITH. And acts of violence, I have done them, too. His head admittedly, I had to saw, and hack, it was an ugly act, the sound of it will live with me until I die, but no, that's nothing. *(Pause.* THE WOMAN *looks at her)*.
THE WOMAN. Then I don't see why —
JUDITH. It was a crime.
THE WOMAN *(pause)*. A crime? And the war Holofernes made against our infant state? Was that not a crime also? And the extermination of our people which he swore to do, the scattering of our tribe, was that not also, crime? Small crime you did, creeping, insect of a crime. Microbe of a crime. Come to Jerusalem and be worshipped for such a crime. I owe you the lives of all my grandchildren. I kiss you, criminal. *(She kisses her)*.
JUDITH. I spoke desire to him. She heard. Did I not utter such desire that —
THE SERVANT. Even I was —
JUDITH. She was thrilled, and he, too —
THE SERVANT. He looked at her and stood away — when she was naked — stood away —
THE WOMAN. Do I need to know this ...!
THE SERVANT. They sat naked, and apart. Intolerable, and wonderful! They looked, they drank and ate the sight of one another naked, the air was solid with their stares —
THE WOMAN. I think, enough, don't you?
JUDITH. You see, I did desire him.
THE WOMAN. The ironies! So it was not entirely acting, nor entirely sacrifice ...
JUDITH. By no means, no.
THE WOMAN. We are human. Or maybe, animal.
JUDITH. And the Israelites, I quite forgot the Israelites.
THE WOMAN. I can imagine ...
THE SERVANT. No, you can't.
JUDITH. I thrived on him. I was in such a heat.
THE WOMAN. They say he was a handsome man.

JUDITH. Not in the least.
THE WOMAN. No?
JUDITH. Even his breath I longed to breathe. And take him in me, head and shoulders also, if I could.
THE WOMAN *(pause)*. It seems very satisfactory to have found, on a mission for the state, such private pleasure —
JUDITH. **Oh, I hate this pleasure!**
THE WOMAN. Listen, I come here not to be regaled with —
THE SERVANT. Shut up, she is telling you —
THE WOMAN *(turning on her)*. **And you.**
JUDITH *(pause)*. I could not have cared if he dripped with my father's blood, or had my babies' brains around his boot, or waded through all Israel.
THE WOMAN. You were obsessed. And in my opinion this makes your triumph greater, an epic of will and the supremely patriotic act. Even tragedy. Come to the city and tell this, I'll be by you. *(She smiles)*. Judith ... *(She extends a hand)*. My dear ... *(Swiftly, JUDITH draws a sword and slices off the proferred hand. A scream)*.
THE SERVANT. Oh, now you've done it!
THE WOMAN. **AAAAAAHHHHHH!**
THE SERVANT. Oh, now you've really done it!
THE WOMAN. **AAAAAHHHHHHH!**
JUDITH. I cut the loving gesture! I hack the trusted gesture! I betray! I betray!
THE WOMAN. Get me to — some hand man — quick! *(THE SERVANT staggers out with THE WOMAN)*. **Hand** ... *(THE SERVANT rushes back, picks up the hand and puts it in a cloth. She hurries away)*.

*THE PHILOSOPHICAL LIEUTENANT
AND THE THREE VILLAGE WOMEN*

CHARACTERS

OFFICER
FIRST WOMAN
SECOND WOMAN
THIRD WOMAN
CORPORAL

A hot day. An OFFICER *seated in a canvas chair, his eyes closed.* THREE WOMEN *enter in peasant costume of the region. They abase themselves.*

OFFICER. *(His eyes unopened).* I see you. You have gone down on your knees, and your white foreheads touch the dirty ground. You think nothing of your costume, which is grey with dust. This morning, you took the garments from your wardrobe, washed and ironed them, and picked fresh flowers from the mountain side. Not since your wedding day have you been so pristine and immaculate. *(He open his eyes).* Is this the national dress? I am not acquainted with the peasant costume of this region. Do rise, I am the lieutenant of the battery and not a god, though secretly perhaps I think I am a god, for reasons you need not concern yourself with. *(They rise).* I have every intention of demolishing the village and all the virgins in the continent and all the petticoats however perfectly embroidered would not stop me but — *(He gestures with his hand).* Plead. I am not so arrogant as to ban your pleading, notwithstanding it could not move me, not a jot.

FIRST WOMAN. My first child was born blind for God knows what sin. In the village he has found work among the cattle who love his voice. The animals pity him and yield more milk to his fingers than any others. If the village is destroyed, he will wander, fall into ditches, and die.

OFFICER. On the contrary, the destruction of the village will be the making of him. You describe a rare gift which any farmer would be glad to hire. He is losing precious opportunities in such a small place, where he remains only to satisfy your charity. You oppress him by your kindness, have you never considered that? No, when the battery fires, it will liberate the blind herdsman. If, as you say, he has such power over animals, they will help him out of any ditch.

SECOND WOMAN. It's obvious you can't be moved by pity, so I won't list the cripples or the hours I spent tying in the thatch. I won't tell you of the thousand hours we put into the sinking of the well, digging the drain to stop the main street flooding, the labour the women went to embroidering the church, or the carving the men did on the altar, no, nor even the trouble we went to building the little gaol, no, this recitation could not touch you so I only add, if you believe yourself to be a god, and at this moment, we accept you as god, however ugly your face and dirty your uniform, shouldn't gods perfect their souls, polish their consciences and be altogether better than the common infantry whose raping we, whose blinding we, must get accustomed to since our troops are gone?

OFFICER. I am afraid you have a narrow view of deity, which I assert is not to do with virtue but only with truth. I think when I feel myself most superhuman, it is in this way, that I discharge myself of all pity and responsibility and recognize the only laws are those of history, or, to put it very simply, I have a house in the capital and we must win this war or my ability to think in comfort and in peace will be terribly impaired. It was clever of you, and subtle, to seek to persuade me by appealing to my love of my own soul, but gods are by definition, above conscience. It is you mortals who must grapple with that one.

THIRD WOMAN. You can fuck me if you want. *(Pause.* THE OFFICER *gets up and walks around, contemplatively).*

OFFICER. I think you are only offering me what, on the one hand, I can simply take. And on the other, something my philosophic nature has subdued.

THIRD WOMAN. You can't take my acquiescence, on the one hand, and on the other, I can see from your trembling lip, you haven't subdued anything.

OFFICER. What kind of bargain would it be, between a god and a mortal? I admit your willing submission would make our union qualitatively different from one achieved by force, and I admit too, your observation that even the most stringent mind cannot suppress the cry of future generations who already send my blood pounding, **Don't lift your skirt**, but I have to say I should enjoy you and still wreck the village, what's my bond worth? A god doesn't respect bargains of that sort. *(Her skirt falls).* So now, by my honesty, I have deprived myself of three satisfactions any normal man would leap at — the satisfaction of showing pity to the weak, the satisfaction of festooning my soul, and the satisfaction of having a child by a woman I shan't see again. You see, I am not corrupted by power! I must be a god! And if you've finished, I will tell the corporal to begin moving the people out. *(Pause.* THE WOMEN *take knives from their skirts).* Ah, now that is desperation itself! And scarcely an argument.

FIRST WOMAN. You have more words than us, you will win all the arguments. We have to save the village and logic's a bastard or we would not be in this war. When we have cut your throat we will go to the corporal and cut his. And having cut his ... etcetera ... down to the regimental spaniel. And having buried you and thrown the guns off the cliffs, we'll watch the crops grow thicker round your pit.

OFFICER. May I expose the fallacy in this?

SECOND WOMAN. You are talking for your life and we are deaf.

OFFICER. I have no option. It is the purpose of my life to think, and to express truth, for example, the truth that soldiers are like wasps round jam, in putting one under the knife you only draw others, and instead of losing the village, you also forfeit life.

THIRD WOMAN. We are the village, and the village is us.

FIRST WOMAN. What you say is true, but we still do it.

OFFICER. You possess a truth, and refuse to act on it? This bewilders me.

THIRD WOMAN. For a man like you, to die bewildered can't be a bad

thing, and we might have both enjoyed that fuck ... *(They crowd round him, and murder him)*.
CORPORAL. Hey ... ! *(They flee. THE CORPORAL runs in with a gun)*. Hey ... ! *(He runs after them. The sound of three shots)*.

NOT HIM

CHARACTERS

A WOMAN
A SECOND WOMAN
THE MAN

A WOMAN *waits for a man. A* SECOND WOMAN *waits with her.*

SECOND WOMAN. Shh!
WOMAN. Not him.
SECOND WOMAN. Could be.
WOMAN. Not him.
SECOND WOMAN. His horse.
WOMAN. But he is not the rider.
SECOND WOMAN. Unless he's changed.
WOMAN. Or I have.
SECOND WOMAN. His step!
WOMAN. He limps ...
SECOND WOMAN. A wound?
WOMAN. He would not wound ...
SECOND WOMAN. His knock!
WOMAN. Some other imitates it.
SECOND WOMAN. Oh, this is love! This is hunger! You dare not think, you dare not imagine! All these years and you refused anticipation. Proof itself arouses your suspicion! *(A further knock).*
WOMAN. Don't go.
SECOND WOMAN. Why?
WOMAN. Something isn't right.
SECOND WOMAN. What?
WOMAN. Either it is not him, or he isn't himself.
SECOND WOMAN. It is his house!
WOMAN. It was, and I was his woman.
SECOND WOMAN. You are so much in love you dread the slightest difference. You have both changed, but only like two skiffs in a river, swung parallel in the current. *(She goes to answer the knock).*
WOMAN. You will say it's him, but all you will be saying is, it looks like him.
SECOND WOMAN. It has been a long war. Do welcome him. *(She goes.* THE WOMAN *covers her face with a veil.* THE SECOND WOMAN *returns).* I think it's him ...

THE MAN *enters with a heavy sack. He puts down the sack.*

MAN. It was a long war, so the sack is heavy.
SECOND WOMAN. You killed many?
MAN *(looking at the* WOMAN*).* Killed and killed. Sometimes they were

brave, sometimes they were reckless, and sometimes they fled! It was never certain. So we sometimes advanced expecting them to flee, and they assaulted us. And other times, in dread of their reputation, we shuddered before the attack, and then they melted away in the darkness, weeping. This was all apparently without reason. But whether they had been stubborn or turned their backs, we still caught them and beheaded them. So in the bag are the heads of heroes and of cowards, which from which is now impossible to distinguish. And now, a chair for me, if I might sit in my own house. *(THE SECOND WOMAN peers in the bag).*

SECOND WOMAN. It's true! These are all heads!

MAN. What did you think, I'd cheat you with cabbages? *(SECOND WOMAN goes to fetch a chair).* You do not raise your veil, quite rightly. You keep your distance, and quite rightly. I have been patient, so what's the delay of a few hours? *(SECOND WOMAN returns. He sits).* The house is clean. The smell of baking tells me all's well.

WOMAN. And what of their women?

MAN. We raped, of course. And some we murdered, but not often. Their skins were oddly white. As for their villages, they won't forget our visits. Do I babble? I am full of stories and gloat. Say if I bore you, or if I am too loud. Ask her to leave now, I am desperate to talk intimately. *(SECOND WOMAN gets up).*

WOMAN. Don't go.

MAN. Don't go, she says ...! *(He smiles).* You are as cruel as ever.

WOMAN. What became of him?

MAN. Of who?

WOMAN. I am also desperate to make love, but first, what became of him?

MAN *(to SECOND WOMAN).* There have been no men here?

SECOND WOMAN. No one near! Anyway, who was there?

MAN. Troops passed through, I saw their wheeltracks.

SECOND WOMAN. Some did.

MAN. Some dusty officers, with rose red epaulettes. Some manly troopers in collapsed boots.

SECOND WOMAN. She hid.

MAN. A woman must.

SECOND WOMAN. Even from her allies.

MAN. Well hid! And now she aches for a man.

WOMAN. I do ache. And soon I'll show you how, but what became of my husband?

MAN. I am your husband, and if you raise your veil I'll believe you are my wife. Though I could love you now, veil or not, here on the tiles.

WOMAN. The more you talk the more I clamour for your body, but I still ask —

MAN. What is this question?

SECOND WOMAN. She wonders if —

MAN. Is the sack not full enough? The dead not dead enough? *(He goes to the sack, tips it. Heads spill out).* I'll hammer bullet cases through the eyes if she requires it, tell her. I did not maim so many, look, these still have ears, would she prefer I pruned them? I come back, not only having saved the village, not only having defended the frontier but crossed it, over mountain ranges where the shepherds have strange eyes, and punished the enemy in their green valleys, burned their churches and their schools, and now the emperor moves the frontier by a dozen miles, what more can a husband do? Lie down, and I will give you children, fill your belly as I tore open others, give you laughing infants as I skewered others, make you a mother here as I ended maternity elsewhere. *(Pause.* THE WOMAN *raises her veil and kisses his mouth).*

SECOND WOMAN. She desires him, as she did not her first husband.

WOMAN. For a long time I did not recognize you. Your voice has changed, and even your shape. And now you speak long sentences when once you grunted.

SECOND WOMAN. Well, if it's him, I'll leave you.

WOMAN. It's him, though his hair is different and his eyes are brown, not grey. And look, his fingers are so slender!

SECOND WOMAN. I'll leave you. *(She goes out.* THE MAN *goes to reach for* THE WOMAN*).*

WOMAN. Put the heads away! I don't want their eyes to see me naked. *(He thrusts them back in the sack, then goes to undress her).* No! Their gore is on your fingers! *(He grabs a cloth and wipes himself, thrusts it aside and goes to her again).* Wait ... Wait, you smell of death. Quick, to the bath and return as perfect as I am.

MAN. Did any man require such reservoirs of patience?

WOMAN. Anticipation of this moment kept me whole through seven years. If we rush through our feelings it will be all over in a second and I shall have no memory to cherish in my widowhood.

MAN. Widowhood?

WOMAN. To lick and roll around my mind on stagnant evenings —

MAN. **Widowhood?**

WOMAN. Shh! My neighbour will run in —

MAN. No, explain this widowhood —

WOMAN. Shan't you die? Are you immortal?

MAN. One day.

WOMAN *(pause).* Then I'll be your widow. That's all.

MAN *(pause, he smiles).* I made widows.

WOMAN. Yes.

MAN. I made them weep so much in places I shall never even see ...

WOMAN. Good. Let them suffer. Let them weep the sight out of their eyes. Go now, the bath's full. *(*THE MAN *turns).* How beautiful you are. Your hip, and your tense thigh. Nothing is imperfect in you. Nothing offends me, in manner or in speech. *(Pause,* THE MAN *goes out.* THE SECOND WOMAN *enters).*

SECOND WOMAN. Is it — has he —

WOMAN. Oh, God, I am sick with desire!

SECOND WOMAN. Oh, wonderful ...! And is he — has he —

WOMAN. I sent him to wash

SECOND WOMAN. I'll go ...!

WOMAN. No, no, wait with me. I am shaking with wanting him, look at my

fingers — and his nakedness!
SECOND WOMAN. I daren't imagine!
WOMAN. His voice —
SECOND WOMAN. Wonderful voice —
WOMAN. His words, his hunger —
SECOND WOMAN. Wonderful words — *(Pause)*. But is it him? *(Pause)*. It isn't, is it? Not him? *(Pause)*. Shh! He's coming! His unbearable haste! *(She goes out.* THE MAN *comes in)*.
WOMAN. You were swift.
MAN. I didn't linger —
WOMAN. Swifter than —
MAN. I didn't lie —
WOMAN. Your skin is —
MAN. Damp still — I didn't —
WOMAN. Damp as earth —
MAN. Touch the towel —
WOMAN. Shh!
MAN *(pause)*. What now?
WOMAN *(pause)*. Listen, the heads ...
MAN. The heads?
WOMAN. Mutter.
MAN. Mutter?
WOMAN. Howl!
MAN. I will remove the heads —
WOMAN. No. It's we who must go.
MAN. Go? But —
WOMAN. I know a place —
MAN. **But this is our —**
WOMAN. Not here, though. *(Pause)*. I will take you in another place.
MAN. What other place? There is no other. We are peasants not landlords, what place ...!
WOMAN. I know one. Where I would rather take you.
MAN *(pause)*. No. Here and now.
WOMAN. No. There and soon.
MAN. **What is this ...!** *(She looks at him. Pause)*. Very well. The meadow if you want. The barn if you want. The stable by all means. *(They leave. Pause.* THE SECOND WOMAN *enters. She sits. She waits.* THE WOMAN *returns)*.
WOMAN. I am pregnant.
SECOND WOMAN *(happily)*. Yes, I believe you are!
WOMAN. Oh, yes. His desire reached so far, and his splash was such a wave. I have a child or nothing is true.
SECOND WOMAN. And did he yell?
WOMAN. He cried out with the awful cry of disbelief that all men make, and his eyes were searching for their focus ...
SECOND WOMAN *(pause)*. You have killed your husband ...
WOMAN. Shh ...
SECOND WOMAN. You have —

WOMAN. Shh ... *(Pause. She sits).* He thrilled me. Oh, his words of violence, how he thrilled me! And his murders, how they flooded me with desire ...
SECOND WOMAN. It was him ...
WOMAN. It was him. Did he think I was fooled?